Crunch
Crackle Pop
Slime Shop

Annalise Grey & Yue Gageby

Wildling Press
1st Edition
ISBN-13: 9781798511855

Dedications

Yue

This book is dedicated to Emma, Helena, and Sara because you enjoy slime like me and have been my friends since the very beginning. Forever cousins by blood, sisters by heart.

I'd also like to give a shout-out to those on social media who work hard to produce good quality slime videos and inspire people like me.

Annalise

I dedicate this book to the Life Skills students at Benjamin Stoddert Middle School. You guys are awesome, fun, and a joy to have in the library.

Thank you for being you.

Contents

S.L.I.M.E.

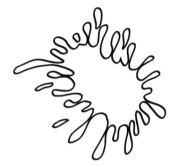

Super stretchy
Lines of lovely colors
Invigorating
Me
Every day

Slime isn't just a toy
a pastime or
something to do when it's rainy outside.

Slime is king
of all things.

Top of the charts fun
good for any time of the day
or night.

Slime is

Loving
Interacting with my
Fabulous creations
Every single day

I'm Mia, by the way.

Mia Ashwood.

Sorry I didn't introduce myself on the first
page
like Mr. Martinez, my fifth grade English
teacher
would tell me to do.

But here I am, saying hi to you
my reader
new friend
partner in slime.

Welcome to my story.

It started with an accident.

I tackled the mountain of
foam like it was Mount Everest
and I,
conqueror extraordinaire,
had no worries in the world.

I had discovered this great new recipe for
butter slime
on Sunshine Queenie's WeBlog channel,
and of course I had to try it
because everyone knows
Sunshine Queenie's recipes are the best.

I stirred the concoction
of glue, shaving cream, and contact solution
until my arm felt like a wet noodle.

Just then, a car horn sounded outside my
bedroom window.

I startled so much I knocked over my gallon of
glue
sending it skidding across the wood floor.

Time slowed down
as three terrible, awful things happened,

one
after
another.

First, a thick ribbon of white
spreads like a monstrous river
trying to devour my floor.

Then Duke, my itchy / twitchy / nervous
puppy
shot like a rocket across the room,
his paws slipping / twisting / spreading
underneath him as he ran through
the flood of glue.

He landed first on his belly then flopped
onto his side as he stopped
by my bedroom door.

My stomach knotted up
as I took in the sight of
such a disaster!

"Mia?"
Mom called from the bottom step.
"Are you okay up there? What happened?"

Icy cold dread washed down my spine.

"Nothing!"
I squeaked.

I grabbed several paper towels
but they only smeared
wide, thin streaks until my floor
became more glue than wood.

"Honey?"
Mom called as her feet hit the stairs.
"What's going on?"

Paper towels stuck
to my arms like big,
ugly white patches.

Duke shook his body
head to tail as if
he had just stepped out of a bath

Little white drops flew every which way
onto my bed
my window
my table
my door and
my mom as she stepped into my room.

My heart dropped to my shoes as
Duke took off running
out the door and down the stairs
knocking Mom off balance.

The *thud* of Mom landing on her bottom wasn't
the worst of it.
The *squish* of glue under Mom's bottom wasn't
the worst, either.
No, the worst was Mom's voice as she turned
to me, with gritted teeth and said,

"No more slime!"

One grounding, two weekends, and lots of dirty socks

I was grounded for forever.

At least, that's what it felt like when
I was up to my elbows
in my older brother, Matt's, dirty sock bin.

He's twelve and has feet that smell like old
Mrs. Blarney's pickles.

(If you've never had old Mrs. Blarney's pickles
I don't recommend trying them; they'll just
make you think of Matt's feet - yuck!)

As punishment, Mom put me in charge of
sorting dirty laundry
    -one load of jeans
    -one load of towels
    -one load for light colors
    -one load for dark colors
    -fifteen loads of Matt's dirty socks

Even Duke stayed away from the laundry
room
while I sorted, washed, rewashed, dried, and
folded

until my back ached and my nose had no more
hairs in it.

I thought laundry was
the worst punishment I could get
until Mom sat me down
at our kitchen table and said,

"You have to get rid of your
slime."

Slime, slime, drowning in slime

The entire world
or maybe just my kitchen
rattled like Mom's announcement
had shifted the earth's
tectonic plates.

Tears bit
at the corners of my eyes.

"I can't throw it away! Slime is my life!"

"Mia,"
Mom sighed and rubbed her temples.
"We're drowning in slime. Look around."

My eyes quickly scanned the kitchen and
found:
    three containers sitting next to the cereal
    five on top of the microwave
    four next to the basket of apples
    seven in a rickety pile near the telephone
    three under a pile of bills, and
    two precariously perched on top of the
window's curtain rod.

(I made a quick mental note of the two sitting
on the curtain rod;
I'd been looking for them for almost a week.)

"Can you give some away?"

"I've worked too hard on it to just give it away.
I've even made my own recipes. They're really
special."

"Honey, I know slime means the world to you
but something's gotta change. You can't be
ungrounded until you figure out how to get rid
of it."

I dragged myself
all the way to my bedroom,
my skin prickling
as if Mom's words had little spikes
stashed in each syllable.

Math

Mom just doesn't understand the value in
one cup of glue
plus
a squirt of shaving cream
plus
a few dashes of contact solution
multiplied by a pinch of glitter
and a few drops of food coloring

which equals
rainy day fun
and
a scientific wonder
made at our kitchen table.

She only believes in what her hands create
with
two cups of flour
plus
one cup of sugar
plus
two eggs and
all the other stuff that turn
a kitchen into a home

She thinks that we're different

when she's baking brownies and cupcakes
and I'm making slime

She doesn't understand,
that in a way,
we're speaking the same language.

Two best friends

Skylar Reynolds and Remi Carroll

Skylar
funny, shy
loves making videos
easily excitable, positive thinker
WeBlogger

Remi
outgoing, popular
loves doing math
easygoing and good natured
genius

When we were five
we made a secret handshake.

up down up down cross over twice
slap snap snap slap snap
cross over fist bump
sing our song

"Lucky pie, cutie duck
driving in a dump truck.
Miss Marple waving hi
catch you later, say g'bye.

At school
we're not Mia
or Skylar
or Remi

We're
MiaSkylarRemi
which sounds like a proper name
if you say it three times fast.

When we're together

When we're together
we are a summer day in motion.

Remi is the cool water
of a bubbling stream.

Skylar is the peaceful quiet
of a sunny afternoon.

And me?
I am the birds in flight,
chirping songs of happiness
at worms and wind.

When we're together
we can tell when something's wrong.

That's just awful

"My mom said I have to throw away my
slime,"
I said, kicking a pebble
across the basketball court.

"What?"
Skylar gasped.

"What?"
Remi echoed her.

I wrapped my arms
around myself.

I told them about
the glue
Duke
the glue all over Duke
the glue Duke sprayed all over Mom
the glue Mom slipped in
and the icing on this sour cake
the piles and piles of Matt's stinky socks.

"I still haven't recovered my sense of smell
completely."

Remi was quiet
which meant she was either mad, sad,
or
working through a math problem
and therefore very, very happy.

It's hard to tell with her sometimes.

Skylar shook her head.
"That's just awful."

"I need to figure out a way to get rid of my
slime. And quick."

Lightbulbs

An idea hit me.
Why did it take me so long?

"That's it!"
I shouted.

"What's it?"
Skylar asked.

"Ladies,"
I said in my best teacher voice.
"I have a plan that is so great, my mom will
have to let me keep making slime **and** it will
make a billion dollars."

"A billion dollars?"
Skylar's bright green eyes nearly popped out
of her head.

She shoved her glasses back up her nose.
"That's an impossible amount of money. How
are you going to do that?"

I cleared my throat and said,
"We're going to open a slime shop."

Remi's hand flew into the air so fast
her dark hair bounced across her shoulders.

"Yes, Remi?"
I pointed to her.

"How are we going to create a slime shop?
We're ten."

"Excellent question; one that will be answered
when we go to the library. This is going to be
top secret."

The library – a place of imagination and wonder… and plotting

"Hi Mrs. Everlock!"

We called to our librarian
as we swooped into the library.

She waved and smiled
as we seated ourselves at our favorite table,
the one closest to the windows that look out
into our school garden.

I grabbed a piece of scrap paper and pencil
from the center of the table.

"To open our shop, we need slime. Lots and
lots of slime."

"You're going to sell your old slime?"
Remi asked.
"What happens when you run out?"

I shrugged.
"I'll make more."

"But your mom banned you from making
more."

"Well... I'm going to change her mind."

Skylar just shook her head.
"Your mom doesn't change her mind."

Remi raised an eyebrow.
"Remember that time you made a boat out of
plastic bins zip-tied together and tried to take it
to the pond? Your mom nearly had a heart
attack and you were grounded for a month."

"Well, yeah but-"

"And remember that time you wanted to build
a tree house out of cardboard and duct tape?
Your mom found out when Duke wouldn't
stop barking at the tree."

"The thing was-"

"You were grounded for the rest of that
summer."

I waved a hand as if shooing away a fly.
"That treehouse was kids' stuff. For the slime
shop, I need to show my mom that I'm
practically grown up and I will do that with a

business plan. But I'm going to need your help."

Skylar and Remi
exchanged a look that said, "Here we go."

It was good enough for me.

The plan

I made a quick list on my paper.

"First, I was thinking we could make videos. Like Sunshine Queenie does but with slime we sell in our shop."

"We could advertise on my WeBlog channel, I have over a thousand subscribers."
Skylar puffed out her chest.
"We review mostly toys and video games so I think slime would be great. Maybe we should do a Slime Saturday vlog series. Dad just bought a new camera so we can shoot better videos outside."

I checked off *Step #3 – Advertise*.

"We also need to brainstorm recipes. I have a notebook with a couple of recipes for butter slime and iceberg slime but I hope you'll help me create some new ones."

Remi clapped her hands together in excitement.

"I make an ocean slime that looks really cool in the container. And when you mix it, it looks like ocean waves in your hand."

I handed her a piece of paper.
"Excellent! Write it down so we can get started."

"How much are we going to sell it for?"
Skylar piped up.

"I'm not sure yet,"
I said.
"That reminds me. *Step #7 – Accounting.* We need someone to be in charge of the money."

Remi flipped her curly locks over her shoulder.
"Um, I have the highest grade in our whole math class so I think I can handle that."

Skylar and I nodded in agreement.

Remi is kind of a math genius.

Last year,
she took first place
in the Mathlete competition
against three other elementary schools.

If anyone can manage money, it's Remi.

"Okay, one last thing: we need a name."

Remi played with a piece of hair.

Skylar stared at her shoes.

"What if we call ourselves the Slime-y Crew?"
I offered.

Skylar shook her head.
"No way! That makes us sound like swamp
creatures."

"How about Slime Time?"
Remi smiled.

I scrunched up my nose.

"The Wonderous World of Slime-Happy
Friends?"
Skylar blurted out.

We all groaned in unison.

"Can I make a suggestion?"

Mrs. Everlock called from her circulation desk. "Make a list of words that come to mind when you think about slime. Start with some descriptions and go from there."

"Mrs. Everlock, you're a genius!"
I declared.

To my friends, I said, "**crunch**. Because iceberg slime crunches and the sound is so satisfying."

Remi tapped her chin.
"I like the way floam slime crackles when you fold it. So… *crackle*. That's a good word to use."

"I just thought of a name,"
Skylar added with a grin.
"Crunch Crackle Pop Slime Shop."

Seal the deal

"I know how to get rid of my slime,"
I told my mom after school.

Her eyebrows knitted
together in that Mom way
that says she's either suspicious, confused, or
smells something gross but can't tell
where it's coming from.

I glanced around the kitchen
in case Matt left his shoes nearby
but I didn't see them anywhere.

"How are you going to get rid of the slime?"
Mom asked.

"I'm going to open a slime shop!"

"A slime shop?"
She choked on her coffee.
"How on earth are you going to do that?"

"I'll make slime and sell it. It's the perfect idea.
I'll make a ton of money!"

Mom sighed.

"Mia, I don't think it works that way. Opening a slime shop would be a lot of work. And we're trying to get rid of slime, not make more."

"Don't you see? I'll get to make all the slime I want and people will buy it which means you don't have to live in a house full of slime. It's a win-win. And Remi and Skylar will help me. They know a lot about slime. We could make our own recipes and Skylar makes videos for her WeBlog channel. She could do advertising. Mom, she has a thousand followers!"

"Have you asked them to help?"
Mom asked.

"Yeah, and they're super excited about it. We spent recess putting this business plan together."

I handed her the list and accompanying diagram we had made earlier today.
"You see? It's a fail-proof, winning plan."

Mom took a few minutes to
look over my notes.

Her left eye twitched slightly and

she tugged at her hair as she read,
so I knew my plan must be good.

"Mia,"
she groaned but didn't
continue her thought.

She ran her hands through her hair
pursed her lips
sighed heavily
handed the paper back to me, then
laid her head on her arms.

"Is that a yes?"
I asked.

After nearly a minute
she gave me a silent nod.

I jumped, shouted,
whooped for joy
and ran out of the kitchen
but not before hearing Mom's wail.

"So much slime!"

Library love

New books, old books, love the smell
spending time with friends
in this special, quiet space

Trade apples for oranges
laughter, fun, and hope
in our most favorite place

High bookshelves, sunny windows
art supplies in hand
shop advertisements to make

The Crunch Crackle Pop Slime Shop
posters almost done
we'll hang them around the school

Mrs. Everlock watched.
"Let me know if you girls need
anything," she said.
"I'll help however I can."

No!

Just around the corner
by Mr. Martinez's classroom
we saw something that made all our jaws
hit the floor.

Isabelle Porter
was putting up
advertisements for a slime shop.

The Bubble Pop Top Shop is taking orders!
See Isabelle in Mr. Green's homeroom.
The best slime around and good prices!

Is that what I think it is?!

"If you're thinking it's a poster for Isabelle's
new slime shop then yes, yes it's exactly what
you're thinking,"
Skylar sighed.

I marched right up to Isabelle and
pointed to the banner.

"What are you doing? You can't open a slime
shop!"

Isabelle raised her chin
as if she's queen of the school
and I, a mere peasant,
am nothing more than an annoyance.

"It's a free country and I can do what I want."

"No, you can't! Opening a slime shop was my
idea and you stole it!"

"It's called living in a free market economy,
Mia."
Isabelle sniffed.

"There can be two slime shops in this school. You don't have a monopoly on slime, you know."

"But it was my idea! I thought of it first! We've been working hard to put this together so you can't just take my idea and call it yours. That's not fair!"

Isabelle placed her
last piece of tape on the edge
of her banner.

"Nobody said life was fair, Mia. Get over it."

My stomach felt
like a nest of writhing snakes.

I watched Isabelle pack up the rest
of her banners, tape, and ribbon
and glide down the hallway,
her cat-like grace on display.

"What do we do now?"

The snakes slithered and crept
up my belly and into my throat
until my voice sounded rough and hard.

Remi pointed to the posters in her hand.
"We should still put those up. I mean, we need
to advertise, right?"

"Let's put our posters far away from
Isabelle's,"
Skylar chimed in.
"That way everybody will see our shop as
something different and they won't get
confused."

We only had a few minutes to work
before lunch was over.

Every time my
gaze traveled around the hall,
I spotted
another advertisement
for Isabelle's shop.

By the time I headed back to class,
the snakes had nestled
at the base of my skull
causing a headache like no other.

The tiger stalks her prey

Isabelle Porter
is like a tiger
with glinting teeth, sharp eyes and
stripes she paints with her
mom's stolen makeup.

Isabelle Porter
stalks her prey when she believes
they're at their weakest,

when they're not looking.
She jumps them from behind when
they least expect it.

Like right now.

Isabelle ruins everything

"I hate Isabelle Porter!"

I was a thundering cloud
as I threw my bedroom door open
after school,
Skylar and Remi on my heels.

"Mia,"
Remi patted my back.
"Isabelle is awful and she totally stole your
idea but…."

"But what?"
I snapped.

Remi glanced at Skylar,
whose eyes seemed glued to her shoes.

"Well,"
Remi grimaced as she turned back to me.
"If Isabelle wants to open her own slime shop,
maybe it's not the end of the world."

"Not the end of the world? Isabelle is going to
ruin everything! She's a backstabbing thief and
she'll find a way to ruin our shop, just wait and

see. Remember that time last year when Mrs. Riviera had us audition for the class play?"

Skylar nodded.
"She told Mrs. Riviera that Cadence's dad left and that Cadence was too heartbroken to perform in a play."

"And what did Mrs. Riviera do?"

"Mia…"

"She told Cadence she didn't have to audition and she'd find something else for her instead. You know how bad Cadence wanted the lead! She practiced every day for a week and Isabelle stole it from her."

"Mia,"
Skylar soothed.
"I know Isabelle is terrible but this is different. I don't think her opening a slime shop is that big of a deal. I mean, yeah, what Isabelle did isn't cool but we can still sell our slime. She might not be real competition anyway. We have different recipes than her."

"We have some really great original recipes,"

Remi agreed.

"I overheard Nate tell Georgia at recess that Isabelle is only selling basic slimes in solid colors. Nothing too crazy."

"So, she won't be much competition," Skylar added.

"You're probably right," I conceded.

"At least, I hope you're right because we've already put a lot of work into this business to let someone like Isabelle Porter ruin it for us."

Slimeber Party

Skylar invited me and Remi over
for a Crunch Crackle Pop slimeber party.

Skylar's dads set up
three tables in a row
in the basement.

One for basic ingredients
like glue and contact solution.

Another for mixing glitter / beads / fun flair.

The last for filling containers, attaching labels,
and signing *thank you* cards.

We spent hours mixing, fixing,
sharing, comparing.

"Ocean slime is my favorite,"
Remi declared
as she sprinkled sand into a set of containers.

"I don't know; the perfect crunch on iceberg is
so satisfying. I just wish it didn't have to sit out
so long to get the dry top layer,"
Skylar sighed.

"No way does iceberg slime compete with butter slime when you get the consistency smooth and spreadable. It's like getting-an-A-on-a-pop-quiz awesome. It took me forever to get it right but now that I have, it's my absolute favorite."

I ran a fresh plastic knife
through creamy butter
slime, red and orange blending,
a lovely sunset.

Before we packed up our shop
and headed up to bed
I gave my friends giant hugs.

"Let Isabelle put up posters all over school,"
I said.
"Our shop has something she doesn't have – a heart."

Success

At recess on Monday
we set up our slime stand
at the corner of the basketball court
closest to the swing set.

Kids swarmed us like they were bees
and we the flowers basking in sunlight.

"Don't forget to follow us on WeBlog!"
Remi shouted to the buzzing crowd.
"We're making our first video this Saturday!"

I spotted Isabelle
under a slide
throwing

daggers

at me
with her eyes.

Surfing waves

I was surfing victory waves
all week as we sold
slime after slime.

I was out of old slime
by Wednesday and by Friday,
running out of new.

I couldn't stop smiling.

Slime Saturday

"Guess what time it is?"
Skylar beamed at the camera.
"It's Sliiiiiime Saturday!"

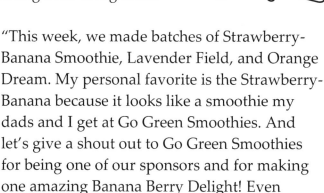

On cue, Remi and I jumped
high into the air
doing a set of big kicks.

"This week, we made batches of Strawberry-
Banana Smoothie, Lavender Field, and Orange
Dream. My personal favorite is the Strawberry-
Banana because it looks like a smoothie my
dads and I get at Go Green Smoothies. And
let's give a shout out to Go Green Smoothies
for being one of our sponsors and for making
one amazing Banana Berry Delight! Even
though it's not edible, the slime in my hands is
an exact color match and smells just as good."

Remi waved a container
in front of the camera
pouring the slime into her shaking hands.

"My, um, favorite out of the three we made
this week is Lavender Fields because, um, it

makes me feel calm when I play with it. And, uh, purple is my favorite color, too."

"And I love the Strawberry-Banana Smoothie too, but since I created the Orange Dream recipe, I'm going to choose that one today," I said, a little too loud.
"I worked on it for almost an hour because I wanted to make slime that swirls like my favorite ice cream."

"All of them have white glue for the base," Skylar explained,
pushing her glasses further up her nose.
"But the Strawberry-Banana Smoothie has three drops of fragrance, three drops of food coloring, and water with a little corn starch. Adding the cornstarch makes it thicker and gives it a softer, smoother texture."

"One piece of, um, advice,"
Remi cut in.
"Be careful that you don't, um, mix the water and cornstarch first because, um, it can create *oobleck* and that, uh, is hard to mix into the slime."

Odd

It was odd
seeing us in the Slime Saturday video.

Remi wasn't the outgoing, bubbly girl
I've known since we were five.

She looked like a ghost was watching her
through the camera lens.

And Skylar
looked confident, strong in a way she isn't
when surrounded by our classmates.

Like they swapped clothing
and became different people
or
became each other.

But me?

I looked like I downed a pot of Mom's coffee,
ran a mile,
and hadn't slept
in almost a week.

Hmm...

"Remi, you've got to take a deep breath and
stop saying um."
Skylar shook her head as the video ended.

Remi rocked back on her heels, blushing.
"Sorry, I was so nervous. I've never filmed a
vlog before."

"Don't be so nervous,"
I added.
"It's just like talking to one of us."

Skylar pursed her lips.
"Yeah, but you shouldn't be quite so loud. Like
you said, pretend you're talking to one of us
sitting here beside you. The microphone will
pick up what you say without you shouting."

"I wasn't shouting."

Skylar gave me a sideways look.

We all sort of stared
awkwardly at each other,
feeling out of place.

"You make this look so easy, Sky," Remi whispered.

I started to wonder if making videos for Crunch Crackle Pop Slime Shop maybe wasn't such a good idea.

Surprise

By the time Monday rolled around
our video had over 500 views,
254 likes, 47 shares, and
31 comments asking where to buy our slime.

Maybe looking like
an exhausted, highly caffeinated rabbit,
a haunted girl,
and a superstar vlogger
might actually pay off.

My brother Matt

My brother Matt is in middle school
and has feet bigger than his IQ.

He drives me crazy
when he pretends he's mature
because he's two years older.

At breakfast
he explained that slime isn't all that special.
"It's just simple chemistry."

He said it's only "changing chemicals'
properties and adding things to make it look
pretty."

But he also said something
that made me say, "yeah!"

"Crunch Crackle Pop needs a few hashtags.
You know, something catchy."

Maybe his IQ
like his shoes
have grown since
starting middle school.

\#

\#crunchcracklepopslimeshop

\#bestfriends

\#greatideas

\#nevergivingup

Monday

We set up on the court's edge
at recess on Monday
selling slime made for the vlog.

In no time at all
a dozen kids have lined up
to purchase from us.

"Check us out on WeBlog!"
Remi called to the crowd.

"This is the prettiest slime I've ever seen,"
one girl with glasses exclaimed.

Her friends *oohed* and *aahed*
as the slime slid over one
hand into the other.

"It smells like dessert."

"How did you make it?"

"That's totally classified."
Remi put a finger to her lips.

"But I promise we'll share other recipes in our videos so follow us on WeBlog and you can learn how to make other slimes."

"Do you follow Sunshine Queenie?"
A girl with short brown hair asked me.
"She's my favorite. Did you see her video on how different types of glue change the texture of slime? She's a genius."

We dived right into an
in-depth analysis of
Sunshine Queenie's videos and recipes.

Just then, Isabelle Porter appeared
near the back of the crowd.

"What do you think you're doing?"
She snapped.

I shrugged.
"Selling slime."

Isabelle narrowed her eyes at me.
"No, this is my place to sell slime. I claimed it on Friday. You can ask Mr. Martinez. He told me I could have this spot, so you have to go somewhere else."

The roaring buzz of the crowd
fell as silent as a graveyard.

"You don't own this space, Isabelle. We were
here first today. It's not my fault if you didn't
get here in time."

Isabelle clenched her fists.

"Fine,"
she said through gritted teeth.
"Anybody who buys from me instead of from
Mia will get twice as much slime for the same
price. A special discount for my friends."

The silence broke
into a million chattering voices.

"Twice as much? That's a great deal!"

"Isabelle's the coolest!"

Remi
Skylar
and I watched in horror
as the kids followed Isabelle
to the other side of the basketball court.

"Wait!"
Remi called as the last kid turned to leave.

He shrugged once before running off
to join Isabelle's swarm.

The happiness I'd been carrying
flew off into the
brilliant afternoon sky,
taking all my hope with it.

Tiger, Tiger, teeth and claws

Tiger, tiger
teeth and claws,
how she moves
on steady paws.

Sleek and sharp
watch her bite,
stalking birds
day or night.

I've become
the little prey,
easy target
she can slay.

Frustrated

Tears pooled at my eyes.

I ran back inside
and headed for the only place
I could cry in peace.

Mrs. Everlock
poked her head around the book shelf.

"Hey, Mia,"
she said with a cheerful grin.

I threw myself into the nearest
overstuffed chair,
hanging my head in my hands.

"What's wrong?"
Mrs. Everlock set down the stack of books
she'd been putting away and
took a seat in the chair beside me.

I shook my head
turned away,
hid.

"It's okay, Mia,"

Mrs. Everlock soothed.
"I'm a good listener if you want someone to talk to."

"We've been working so hard to get the slime shop started."

Mrs. Everlock passed me a tissue box
from the table in front of us.

"We even stayed up late this weekend to finish a batch of slime. Then today no one bought them! Isabelle just told everyone she'd give them twice as much slime if they bought from her instead."

Mrs. Everlock pursed her lips.
"That's called being ruthless in business, Mia. It doesn't feel fair, does it?"

I shook my head,
wiped my tears.

"My mom let me start the shop because I had a perfect plan."

"Are you worried your mom won't let you make more slime?"

I nodded.

"Have you talked to her about it?"

"No,"
I admitted.
"She'll just get mad at me. And if I fail, she's going to make me get rid of it all, for sure."

"How do you know she won't be proud of you for trying? You've done some great work, Mia. Don't let fear keep you from your dreams."

Mrs. Everlock held up her fist
for a knuckle bump.

"I believe in you."

An alien

I spent the evening
thinking over how to talk to Mom
about the slime shop,
Isabelle, her "sale"
how it's all fallen apart.

"Hey kiddo,"
my brother Matt said
as he messed up my hair at dinner.

He knows I hate it
when he acts like he's so grown up
and I'm a little kid.

I swatted his hand away
and ducked when he tried to mess it up
again.

"Ugh!"
Mom threw her hands in the air.
"Will you both just stop? I'd like to have a nice
quiet dinner, for Pete's sake!"

We didn't say anything for forever.

At least, until Mom cleared her throat

and gestured around her.

"Do you know what this house is missing?"
She asked.

Matt and I glanced around the kitchen
but everything seemed to be
right where we left it.

"Slime!"
Mom smiled.
"The house is officially slime-free. Not a
container in sight. Isn't it glorious?"

Sometimes
I feel like an alien,
a true outsider
even with my family.

Attack

I wandered through the next few days
like a slug in sand.

Remi and Skylar
didn't bring up the slime shop.

We sat
on the swings at recess,
watching Isabelle's fan base multiply
like weeds.

My stomach hurt,
twisted in on itself like
lava bubbled just under my skin.

On our way inside from recess
Isabelle slinked past me
her claws on full display.

"You should stick to playing with slime since
it's all you're good at."

Doubt

Doubt
feels like a weight
when you're already under water.

Like when the world is shrinking
and all you're doing
is sinking.

Gulping down your last breaths of air
clinging to dreams
with nothing to spare.

Trash

I

d
r
o
p
p
e
d

m
y

l
a
s
t

c
o
n
t
a
i
n
e
r

o
f

slime   into   the   trash.

Terrible news

On Monday
I headed to the library for recess.

A young lady with short blond hair
peered up from Mrs. Everlock's
circulation desk.

"May I help you?"

I blinked twice before I realized
she was talking to me.

"Where's Mrs. Everlock?"

The young woman's face fell.
"I'm so sorry, sweetie. Mrs. Everlock will be
out for some time. I'm her substitute, Ms.
Harris."

"Out?" I sputtered. "Is she sick?"

Ms. Harris shook her head.
"No, Mrs. Everlock was in a car accident over
the weekend."

The lava in my belly turned solid.

"Is she okay? When is she coming back?"

Ms. Harris put her hand up
to quiet me and smiled gently.

"She's pretty banged up. I believe she has a
couple of broken ribs, a broken leg, and a nasty
bump on her head but she's tough. She should
be back to school in a few weeks."

"A few weeks?"

My throat felt tight
like a chunk of cooled lava
wedged itself behind my vocal chords.

Ms. Harris nodded.
"It was a bad accident from what I've heard. A
truck didn't stop when it was going through a
traffic light and it hit her. She's lucky, though.
At least she survived."

Library blues

I walked around the bookshelves
but nothing felt the same.

The books seemed dull,
less alive without
someone to love them,
to call them special.

I realized
for the first time
just how much Mrs. Everlock
makes this place home.

Downhill with no brakes

Everything
is

f
  a
    l
      l
        i
          n
            g

a
  p
    a
      r
        t

School daze

No Crunch Crackle Pop Slime Shop
no way to make time stop

Feeling more and more like a ghost
giving up what I love most

Miserable
Inadequate
Ashamed

More teeth and claws

I trudged behind my classmates.

"Not selling slime again today, Mia?"
Isabelle's bite was extra sharp.

I could practically see her whiskers
twitching with glee.

I put my head down
and looked away.

"Did you hide in the library again?"

I bit my lip so I wouldn't cry.

I couldn't let Isabelle win at everything.

"No. Mrs. Everlock isn't here because she was
in a car accident."

Isabelle gasped and stopped walking.
"What?"

Ignoring her,
I kept walking
but a hand stopped me.

I turned to face
The Tiger.

I prepared myself
for her pounce.

But instead
her claws had retracted;
her teeth were normal-sized.

Isabelle looked like
a regular girl
for the first time in ages.

"Mia,"
she said quietly.
"I'm so sorry. I don't know what to say."

"You don't have to say anything. You win.
That's all there is to it."

I gathered up the little bit of pride
I had left,
scooped it up like a new puppy
and held it close
as I walked back to class
alone.

A spark

Mr. Martinez made an announcement.

"Okay, kids. I'm throwing away my lesson
plan for today."

Our class
had been unusually quiet
since Mrs. Chang, the principal
told us about Mrs. Everlock
during morning announcements.

"I know you're all worried about Mrs.
Everlock,"
Mr. Martinez explained.
"So let's talk about it. Let's get it out in the
open and then maybe you'll feel better. Leave
your things at your desk and come have a seat
over in our reading corner."

We made our way to the oversized carpet.

I squeezed in next to Nate and Georgia.

"I talked to Mrs. Everlock last night and she
wanted me to tell you all that she misses you
very much and that she's going to be okay."

"We should do something nice for her,"
Nate said.

"I agree,"
Mr. Martinez smiled.
"What if we all wrote her get-well cards
instead of reading the short story I had
planned? Making a card is *technically* reading
and writing so it's educational, right?"

Mr. Martinez winked at the class
and told Nate
to get out the crayons and colored paper.

He put on music
which is usually not allowed in school.

Then
Mr. Martinez opened a bag of candy
and gave us each a piece
which is *really* not allowed.

He also let us take off our shoes
which is ***absolutely no-way at all*** not allowed.

Mr. Martinez is awesome like that.

While working on Mrs. Everlock's card,
an idea sparked in my brain.

The spark became a flame
burning brighter and brighter
as I colored
until I couldn't contain it any longer.

I asked Mr. Martinez for the hall pass
and headed straight for Mrs. Chang's office.

This, I thought as I knocked on the principal's
door, *might be my greatest idea yet.*

Hope

"Come in, Mia."
Mrs. Chang waved to me.

I sat down in the big chair
in front of Mrs. Chang's
polished wood desk.

I'd never been to
the principal's office before.
My stomach did little flips.

There were pictures of
Mrs. Chang and two kids who
look like her climbing
a steep, rocky cliff
safety ropes hooked to their belts.

Another picture,
showed Mrs. Chang jumping from
an airplane, parachute
strapped to her back.

My mouth fell open.

Our principal
is cool. Maybe a little

crazy but still cool.

Mrs. Chang laughed out loud.
"I take it you haven't done much skydiving,
huh Mia?"

"No, I haven't. It looks terrifying."
I breathed.
"And also fun."

"It's quite an experience, for sure."
Mrs. Chang smiled.
"But I suspect you're here to talk about
something else, am I right? What can I do for
you, Mia?"

I cleared my throat and
straightened my shoulders.

Sounding professional is
important in times like these.

"I want to hold a fundraiser,"
I said.
"For Mrs. Everlock."

"A fundraiser, you say?"
Mrs. Chang tapped her chin with a finger.

"That's very generous of you, Mia. How do you propose we host this fundraiser?"

"With a carnival."

"A carnival?"
Mrs. Chang's brows shot upward.
"A carnival would be very difficult to put on, especially with such short notice."

My heart dropped.
"Oh."

"But I will let you in on a little secret. It turns out that our school's Parents And Teachers group had a similar idea just this morning."

My heart thudded against my chest.
"Really?"

"Yes! In fact, I met with the PAT president this morning to start planning a family fun night here at school to raise money for Mrs. Everlock. You see, Mrs. Everlock is very much loved and many of us were devastated to hear about her accident. The PAT and I are going to start planning the event later this week."

"That's amazing! Thank you, Mrs. Chang!"

She grabbed a pen from her desk,
scribbled a quick note.
"Mia, when you get home, can you have your
mom call me here at school? We could use
some students to help us put this together.
Maybe you could be on the planning
committee?"

Joy and excitement
stomped down the snakes,
pushed back the lava
and took an axe to
all the monstrous feelings
that had popped up like weeds.

Hope
had set me free.

Here we go

Mom was thrilled
I had found a passion for something
that wasn't slime.

She knew
I came up with the idea
for a fundraiser
and had the guts to ask my principal.

She knew
the Parents And Teachers (and me!)
have started planning a
Summerville Elementary
Family Fun Night.

She knew
we'll have face painting
games
a hayride around the school grounds
raffles and prizes
and people selling stuff like
artwork and jewelry.

What Mom didn't know is that
I had asked the PAT committee to let
Crunch Crackle Pop Slime Shop

have a slime station
next to the family games area.

They told me **yes!**

Renewed

I feel like a bird
holding the wind in my feathers.

I feel weightless,
in love with the sweet spring air.

I have become
something greater than I've been.

I want to carry
my dreams up, up, up to the sky.

And drop little
bits of stars here and there for
everyone to see.

School craze

All the kids at school
were going crazy
over the Family Fun Night.

In art
we made decorations
to hang on the walls.

In chorus, we practiced songs
we'll perform for our parents.

At recess, the hive swarmed around
Remi, Skylar, and me.

We spread the word that
the Crunch Crackle Pop Slime Shop
would donate all
money we made from slime sales
to Mrs. Everlock's fund.

"Are you going to make another video soon?"
One girl asked.

"Will you share some recipes?"
Another piped up.

"If you help us go viral!"
I said with a grin as wide as the ocean.

Ready, set, go!

Skylar's dad started recording
when she gave him a thumbs-up.

"Welcome back to Crunch Crackle Pop Slime
Shop! I know it's been a little while since our
last video. We've had a lot of ups and downs
here lately but we're officially back!"

Remi, Skylar, and I
cheered and stretched a giant batch
of neon green, snot-looking slime.

It jiggled and made a *sloosh* sound.

"Today, we're talking about our first slime
recipes. Did you know that my first ever slime
was a soap slime?"
Skylar asked me.

"I didn't know that,"
I replied.
"I've never tried a soap slime. Aren't they hard
to make?"

"Not really but it takes forever. Papa and I
gathered all the leftover soap pieces in the

house and soaked them in about two cups of water. It took a couple of days but when it was done, the slime was pretty and I used it at bath time."

"My first slime was white glue-based,"
Remi said, her voice still a little shaky.

She glanced at the camera
before turning to me.

"Remember when your mom brought that kit home and we made a mess in your kitchen?"

"Oh yeah, the floam slime."
I laughed.
"It was such a disaster! Floam beads went everywhere and my mom swept the floor six times in one day. She still gets mad when I talk about it."

"Can we make a floam slime for the next video?"
Remi whispered to Skylar.

Skylar beamed at the camera.
"Sure. If you'd like to see us make a floam slime for our next video, click on the comments

below and let us know. And don't forget, Crunch Crackle Pop Slime Shop is open for business so if you want to buy the slimes we make, check out the link in our description."

We waved slime hands at the camera.

"Remember, all money is going to help our school librarian, Mrs. Everlock. We want to raise as much as we can so share this video, follow us, and get the word out. We're back and creating new and exciting slimes that are sure to brighten your day."

Skylar's dad held his hand up
then counted down from five.

"That's a wrap, girls. Well done."

Trending

Our video went live
and by bedtime
it had been shared over two thousand times.

When we awoke for breakfast
the shares had doubled.

By lunchtime
we'd reached over nine thousand.

Crunch Crackle Pop Slime Shop
had gone viral.

#**viral**

#crunchcracklepopslimeshop

#itwasthebestofslimesitwastheworstofslimes

#mrseverlock

#schoollibrariansrock

#slimersunite

One thought
kept circling my brain
like a sparrow
hoping to find a perch

#birdandtigercallatruce

Friends?

I spotted Isabelle
sitting alone under the monkey bars.

She played with her shoe laces
and didn't look up
when I said hi.

"Can I sit here?"

She shrugged
but didn't say anything.

"I was thinking,"
I started then paused,
trying to remember what I'd practiced
last night before bed.
"We could use some help with the slime
station during the Family Fun Night."

She didn't look at me right away
but I knew she was listening.

"Look, we can keep fighting and being stupid
or we could do something really great. What if
Bubble Pop and Crunch Crackle Pop work
together?"

"I thought you hated me,"
she whispered.

I rolled a blade of grass
between my fingers.

"I thought *you* hated *me*. You can be pretty
mean, you know."

She sniffed
as a tear slipped down her cheek.

"I guess I was jealous because you have a lot of
friends. And you always get the best grades!
You don't even try and you're, like, perfect."

I laughed,
shaking my head.
"Wow, that's crazy because I'm not perfect at
all. I can't even make a slime shop work. And
nobody's impressed with my real talent."

Isabelle cocked her head to the side.
"What's that?"

"I can burp the alphabet."

Family Fun Night

The parking lot was packed.

Car lines stretched up
and down
the streets around
Summerville Elementary.

I pressed my nose to the car window,
watching families travel in packs
toward the school.

Toward my school.

Mom blew out a whistle as
she circled around to the teacher's lot.

"The doors don't even open for another twenty
minutes and people are already lining up!"

Even Matt showed signs of excitement.

"Hey! Jake and Toby are here! Cool, I'll have
friends to talk to."

Earlier tonight,
Mom threatened him with grounding

if he didn't "straighten out" his attitude
about coming to the event.

My chest squeezed a little
as we burst through the front lobby doors.

Student artwork, balloons, and streamers
hung in pretty rows along the walls.

Lights flashed to the beat of music
from the DJ stand in the corner.

On our way to the slime station,
we passed artists and jewelry makers,
a face painter and other local businesses
advertising everything from selling houses to
veterinary services.

"Mia,"
Mom stopped, her eyes going wide.
"Look at how the community has come
together to raise money for Mrs. Everlock."

"I know. Since our video went viral, everyone
has been calling the school to ask how they can
help. Even the mayor! She's supposed to give a
speech tonight, but I don't remember what
time."

Mom's mouth fell open
as if she was waiting
for the right words to jump in.

"This…,"
she breathed.
"This is incredible, Mia."

I gave Mom my best smile.
"Wait until you see our slime station."

Crunch Crackle Pop Slime Shop

Skylar, Remi, Isabelle, and I
were allowed to skip our last class today
so we could start setting up the slime station.

Our last video received
so many shares, likes, and comments
that the local news station called the school.

They said they were sending a reporter
to cover the Family Fun Night
and hoped to interview our principal.

Mrs. Chang decided
Crunch Crackle Pop Slime Shop
should have a special spot
at the back of the gym.

There,
just past the hot dog and soft pretzel stands,
along the back wall of
Summerville Elementary
hung a giant banner.

Crunch Crackle Pop Slime Shop
All proceeds go to support
our favorite librarian, Mrs. Everlock!

When the doors opened
a short time later,
Remi, Skylar, Isabelle, and I were swamped
with customers.

We sold glitter slimes
pastel slimes
ocean slimes
candy slimes
and more.

Guest of honor

I was telling a third grader
in Mr. Olson's class
how to tell if slime is set
when the gym erupted
in applause.

Every head turned
to see who or what
was causing the reaction.

Mrs. Everlock,
in a big wheelchair
appeared by the door to the gym.

"Mrs. Everlock!" I squealed

The man behind her
pushed her through the crowd.

She waved,
giving the gym a warm smile.

Then
she headed straight for us.

Wow!

"I don't even know what to say except thank
you!"
She wiped a few tears from her face.
"Thank you, a million times over, Mia. You
and the PAT. You have no idea what this
means for me."

She was covered in those casts
doctors use for broken bones
so I couldn't give her a hug.

Instead,
Remi, Skylar, and I
(and now Isabelle, too!)
taught her our secret handshake.

She let out a brief laugh
but I could tell it hurt her.

"You girls are really incredible,"
she said.
"You should be proud of yourselves. And be
proud of Crunch Crackle Pop Slime Shop."

S.L.I.M.E

Satisfying end to a successful night
Lively friends, time well-spent
I'm happier than I've ever been
Mom says she understands now
Everything's going to be A-okay

Crunch Crackle Pop Slime Shop's Slimatory recipes & notes

Mia's basic white slime

¾ cup white glue
1 fluid ounce glue
2 fluid ounces water
About 1 teaspoon baking soda

Mix ingredients. Add a little contact solution (activator) and mix. Add more contact solution if needed to reach desired consistency.

Once mixed well, take the slime out of the bowl or cup you're mixing in and continue to mix and stretch by hand.

Make sure the slime doesn't stick to the cup or bowl you're using to mix before you take it out.

Add your favorite flair such as beads, glitter, sand, and more!

Mia's favorite jiggly slime

½ cup white or clear glue
¼ cup water
2 tablespoons baby oil
About 1 teaspoon baking soda

Mix ingredients. Add a little contact solution (activator) and mix. Add a tiny amount of water until desired jiggliness. You might have to add a little more contact solution if it gets too sticky.

Once mixed well, take the slime out of the bowl or cup you're mixing in and continue to mix and stretch by hand.

Make sure the slime doesn't stick to the cup or bowl you're using to mix before you take it out.

Add your favorite flair such as beads, glitter, sand, and more!

Tips & tricks

To add color, start with your favorite food color or paint or pigment.

Food coloring clear slime – add one or two drops to start.
Food coloring white slime – add two or three drops to start. Add more for darker colors.

Coloring clear slime with paint – add one tiny squirt to start. Add another squirt of paint for darker colors.

Coloring white slime with paint – add three squirts to start. Add another squirt or two of paint for darker colors.

Coloring slime with pigment – start with ½ teaspoon to start. Add another ½ teaspoon for more pigmented colors.

Tips for using coloring of any kind

Wear old clothes that can get stained up and don't forget to use plastic under your slime station. Most food colorings, paints, and pigments will stain clothes, skin, and surfaces.

Gloves are always a good idea!

Keep your slimatory clean so you don't get random stuff in your slimes!

ADD YOUR OWN RECIPES AND NOTES ON THE FOLLOWING JOURNAL PAGES!

RECIPES & NOTES

RECIPES & NOTES

RECIPES & NOTES

RECIPES & NOTES

RECIPES & NOTES

RECIPES & NOTES

_____

_____

_____

_____

_____

_____

_____

_____

_____

_____

_____

_____

_____

_____

_____

_____

_____

_____

_____

_____

_____

_____

_____

_____

_____

_____

RECIPES & NOTES

RECIPES & NOTES

RECIPES & NOTES

RECIPES & NOTES

Acknowledgements

Yue

I'd like to thank Mommy for being the best mommy in the world and being super supportive. I'd also like to thank Daddy, Grandma, Miss Erin, Mr. Robert, Emma, and Sara for enjoying slime with me and getting excited about new recipes.

Annalise

I want to say thank you to my husband, Shawn, who listened to me and Yue plotting, discussing, dissecting, and getting excited about a book about slime, of all things. (Because we aren't already up to our eyeballs in slime… nope, Yue and I had to write a book about it as well.) So thank you for all your support! Also, I have to give a shout-out to my son, Nick, for all the hugs and encouragement.

About the authors

Annalise Grey is a Pennsylvania native, dreamer, explorer. She writes because she likes talking to the voices in her head. Her work has been featured in Tiny House Magazine, Anti-Heroin Chic Literary Magazine, and Micro Fiction Monday Magazine.

You can find more info on her and her books at www.ramblingsofatiredmind.com.

Yue Gageby is a self-proclaimed slime expert who specializes in creating new recipes and making messes in her slimatory. She loves reading, shopping, making videos, hanging out with her dog Hazel, and spending time with her family. This is her first book.

Follow Crunch Crackle Pop Slime Shop on Instagram. @crunchcracklepopslimeshop